whenever there is danger send for...

Kung-Fu
Pigs

Scholastic Children's Books,
Commonwealth House, 1–19 New Oxford Street,
London, WC1A 1NU, UK
A division of Scholastic Ltd
London ~ New York ~ Toronto ~ Sydney ~ Auckland
Mexico City ~ New Delhi ~ Hong Kong

First published in the UK by Scholastic Ltd, 2004

ISBN 0 439 96856 9

Printed and bound by Nørhaven Paperback A/S, Denmark

10 9 8 7 6 5 4 3 2 1

Kung-Fu Pigs

The Temple of Ghosts

Keith Brumpton

SCHOLASTIC

THE LO-FAT HILLS

THE CAVE
WITH
NO NAME
Home of the

CHIN CHIN
(Rinki's home)

PORKAIDO

KNOCKNEEDO

The Pork-i
Kingdom

BRIDGE OF THE
SEVENTH GOLDFISH

NO-PEKIN
Capital city, home to
our great and noble emperor

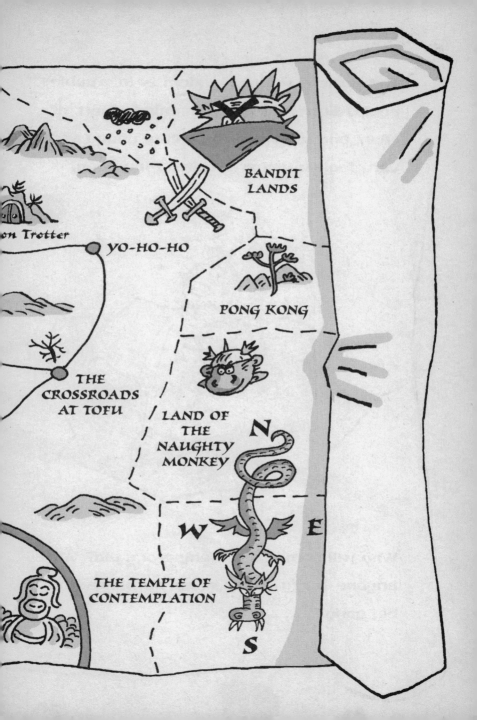

The ancient Pork-i kingdom is in trouble again. Surrounded by enemies, short of cash, and ruled over by a very young and very foolish emperor called Ping-Pong.

Who will come to the emperor's aid? Will anyone hurry along when he bangs the big gong?

The Temple of Ghosts

Translated from the original Pork-i manuscript by Keith Brumpton

PROLOGUE

I am the old and wise Oinky No Ho, venerable priest of Wu-Dah-Ling, and my knees make a strange noise when I walk. I am here to tell of the time when the Kung-Fu Pigs, those famous fighters, answered the emperor's call and agreed to travel to the Temple of Ghosts. Yes, that same Temple of Ghosts where many brave pigs have vanished without trace. In this tale you will meet strange spirits of the night, treacherous villains, and pigs with mild frostbite.

But the shadows grow long, and so, honourable stranger, let us begin...

CHAPTER 1

"The brightness of his treasure can make a rich pig blind."

Confuse-us, 3rd century philoso-pig

The fine palace of Ping-Pong was a miserable place that morning. Though the winter sunshine glittered, you could cut the atmosphere in the throne room with a sharp chopstick. And why were spirits so low?

The emperor was down to his last million — that's why.

He'd been going through his accounts with a fine comb, and there was no doubt about it.

"But they are also half full," answered one of his courtiers, whose name the emperor could never remember.

This remark cheered the emperor for a moment, until he realized that this was the same thing!

He was a young pig who loved treasure. And he knew how to spend it. Fast. Indeed, the main reason why the emperor was so short of funds was due to his own foolishness.

Ping-Pong spent the kingdom's wealth on himself: on gold slippers; on a silver comb; on a silver shaving set even though he wasn't old enough to shave.

But now, with less cash to spend, he was having to make cutbacks: seven courses of lunch instead of ten, two servants to help him get dressed instead of four.

The royal nanny, Manki Hanki, arrived, and sat herself at the foot of the throne. She had been Ping-Pong's nanny since he was a little piglet and he still couldn't get through the day without her.

"What have you there, nanny?" asked Ping-Pong, in his squeaky voice.

"It is a scroll," she answered.

"I can see that!" snapped the young emperor, impatiently. "What does it say?"

Manki Hanki unfurled the parchment to its full length.

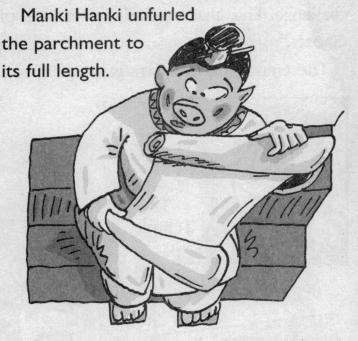

"This, oh noble emperor, Lord of the eight armies and twelve navies, and Ruler of the mighty river Tchang, Prince of—"

"Yes, yes! I know who I am! What does it say?!"

"This may be the answer to your financial troubles," smiled the emperor's nanny. "The scroll tells of an ancient challenge. The challenge of the Temple of Ghosts."

The emperor's courtiers gasped.

Ping-Pong's nanny sat closer
and began to read the scroll.

She told of how any pig who could spend
a night in the Temple of Ghosts and live to
see the dawn would be rewarded with
fabulous treasure.

"Treasure!" beamed
the emperor, clapping
his fat little trotters
together. "Fabulous
treasure. We like
that!"

Ping-Pong thought that this might be the answer to all his prayers. "Where is this Temple of Ghosts?" he squeaked.

"It is in the far south of the kingdom, in a land of snow and ice," said Manki Hanki. "But alas, no one has ever succeeded in winning this challenge."

"Those who have tried have either vanished or gone mad," Manki Hanki declared, and she rolled her eyes dramatically.

"That doesn't matter," answered Ping-Pong, calmly.

Manki Hanki was very impressed. "Oh, my brave little soldier! Would you really risk spending a night inside the Temple of Ghosts to win the treasure?"

The reply came swiftly back. "Of course not, silly nanny! I'm far too delicate for that sort of thing. No ... I shall send for the Kung-Fu Pigs! They can spend the night there on my behalf!"

And with that, the emperor got to his feet (which wasn't very far because he only had little legs) and ordered that Oinky No Ho be summoned and his great gong sounded.

CHAPTER 2

"True friendship is the one treasure that can never be spent."

Ti-Phu, poet, 4th Dynasty

Oinky No Ho's gong was very large. It was the size of two pigs laid end-to-end and then a little bigger still.

The sound of the gong travelled out beyond the emperor's gardens (where there was not a weed in sight), over paddyfields, across dense, snow-dappled woods, and over muddy country lanes, to where the Kung-Fu Pigs – the heroes of our story – were going about their business.

That gentle and good-natured priestess, Dinki, was seated on a bench inside the Great Hall of the Leaky Temple.

She was playing chess with a fellow priest.

And what of the second of the Kung-Fu Pigs, that hot-blooded young pig known as Rinki? He wasn't playing chess. No, that wasn't his style at all. Rinki was busy practising his sword-fighting skills with his cousin, Chunki.

"Tching! Tching!" The sound of their swords rang round the icy barn.

Two-dragon slice...

And then...

Parry with the No-Fun Defence.

Hah!

Rinki was determined he would be ready whenever the emperor called. Which was just as well...

But of course there remained one more Kung-Fu Pig: that samurai fighting machine known to the world as Stinki. What was occupying his thoughts as the great gong sounded?

Mmm ... just a few more potatoes ... yum yum...

DONG!!!

Food, of course! Stinki peered into his wok and licked his lips hungrily. Though he would have run through walls for the emperor, our friend Stinki was still just a little miffed to have to abandon his lunch.

Curses! Not even time for a mouthful!

So it was that each of the Kung-Fu Pigs prepared to answer the call. And now, each in turn hurried towards the great capital city of No-Pekin, where their guru, the wise and noble and slow-moving Oinky No Ho awaited them. And where the emperor's piggy banks were only half full...

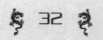

CHAPTER 3

*"Better to follow the road
with one who knows it,
than to stumble on alone."*
Ho Ho Ho, poet, Dong Dynasty

Early the next morning, our three heroes
arrived at the palace.

"Greetings, honourable master," began
Rinki, on entering the frost-covered garden
of Oinky No Ho. All three pigs bowed low.

"What's happened?" asked Stinki, excitedly. "Are there more wolves to fight?"

Wise Oinky No Ho replied with a shake of the head and bade them follow him indoors. It was hard work following Oinky No Ho. He moved slower than an elderly snail. Rinki had to walk on the spot to avoid taking the lead. But eventually they reached a sparse room where a fire was lit and three bowls of tea laid out before them.

"Emperor Ping-Pong, our wise and all powerful leader, has asked me to send you on a mission," Oinky No Ho began.

Rinki clenched his fist with delight, for he was a pig who loved adventure.

"But it is a mission of great danger," said Oinky No Ho.

The fire crackled in the hearth.

...And there is a chance none of you will come back alive.

"Cool," whispered Stinki, who loved danger almost as much as his friend Rinki.

Oinky No Ho picked up a slightly battered-looking scroll.

 35

"The emperor has asked you to travel to a place known as the Temple of Ghosts." Dinki stopped sipping her tea and a look of concern crept over her face. "I have heard of this place," she whispered, in worried tones. "It is very dangerous. You must stay for a whole night inside the temple in order to win a prize of treasure."

Treasure? Cool!

"This will be easy," Stinki laughed. "Who's frightened of ghosts? There's no such thing!"

Wise Oinky No Ho shook his head with disbelief. "Oh, impetuous Stinki, you have much to learn. These ghosts do exist. And they are not just any ghosts ... they are of the hopping variety. If you are to survive this mission then you must listen very carefully to what I am about to tell you..."

The old man settled himself in a chair and began. "The temple ghosts are the most dangerous type of ghosts one can ever meet," he said, eyeing his pupils sternly.

Oh, I'm *so* frightened.

"Quiet, foolish samurai," said Dinki. "We must find out what we can about these ghosts. Will you two ever learn?"

C'mon, Dinki! A few spooks don't frighten us.

Oinky No Ho's face grew sterner still. "I had a pupil once, who thought as you do. A brave young warrior called Yu Han Mi. He was a fine swordsman like young Rinki here. And strong, like you, Stinki. But what he did not know is that neither strength nor skill with a sword will ever defeat a hopping ghost."

Hopping ghost? Hehehe!

Master, what are these hopping ghosts?

A hopping ghost is an undecayed corpse, whose soul has not yet left for another world.

But what makes it hop?

"The ghost does not want to be buried in an unfamiliar place, so it will try to hop home," said Oinky No Ho.

"Their joints are stiff as wood, but sometimes they can fly too. Their most lethal weapon is their fingernails, which are very long and extremely sharp.

During the day they hide in coffins or caves, but at night they begin to emerge ... looking for trouble..."

Is there any way of defeating them?

Not with ordinary weapons.

But I can give you some things that might help...

Here, take these ... they are all lucky charms that will help you defeat the ghosts...

an eight-sided mirror

a straw broom

long-grained rice

...and a red and yellow death blessing. The words of the blessing are written on the other side. Be careful to learn it well.

This is crazy!

I've never gone into battle with a broom before! Has old Oinky finally flipped?

Only Dinki seemed impressed.
"Thank you, honourable master. But you have not told us what happened to your pupil, Yu Han Mi?" said Dinki.

CHAPTER 4

"Winter chills the trotters and the water in the trough is frozen."
Chin Chin, wandering minstrel. 847

When Oinky No Ho had finished describing the terrible ghosts that might be awaiting them, the Kung-Fu Pigs looked at one another and then stood up as one.

"Fear not, Oinky No Ho. These temple ghosts don't frighten us!" growled Stinki.

The priestess Dinki nodded in agreement. "We will do our best."

As they walked across the white-frosted garden, the emperor himself appeared on the balcony of his Great Palace in order to wave them off. He was standing on a little set of steps to help him see over the railing.

"Succeed in your mission and I will reward you well," he called out, squeakily.

Rinki bowed low and then answered for his companions. "Serving Your Majesty will be reward enough."

"Phew!" thought the emperor, secretly. "I didn't really want to give them anything … I'm hard-up as it is."

And with that, he went off to count some of his gold coins.

The Kung-Fu Pigs set off on their long and arduous journey. The Temple of Ghosts lay in the far south of the kingdom and after many hours of travel, snow had begun to fall and the road ahead grew slow and steep.

"Are we nearly there yet?" Stinki asked, through chattering teeth.

Rinki tried to cheer his samurai friend by reminding him that cold weather was great for stoking up an appetite.

"But my trotters are so numb I won't be able to hold my chopsticks!" Stinki complained.

"Perhaps we can stop at a country inn," added Rinki, cheerfully.

Dinki didn't think this was a good idea. "Country inns are dangerous places to stop. All sorts of bandits and ruffians hang around them, waiting to pick off travellers like ourselves. Let us keep going until we reach the temple. I have a prawn cracker we can share."

And so they travelled on. Up hills and down valleys, swapping news and telling tales…

As the light began to fade, Dinki saw something up ahead. "What's that?"

HU'S COUNTRY INN
UNWARY TRAVELLERS
WELCOME

It was a moonless and bitter night, and even Dinki felt like stopping. Rinki and Stinki told her it would be safe at the inn and she was too tired to argue.

The innkeeper was a friendly-looking pig with a wispy beard and eyes so close together they almost met in the middle. His wife showed them to their room.

What brings you strangers to these parts?

Stinki looked
unimpressed.
"How many stars
does this place have?"
"Just the ones you
can see through the
hole in the roof,"
answered their host.

Soon they were all asleep. Stinki dreamt of a fine stew served up with dumplings, and Rinki of a new sword. Dinki didn't dream at all for she was so exhausted by the journey and the cold.

CHAPTER 5

*"Beware the thief in the night.
He is not there for a bedtime story."*
No Li Wei, court official, 2nd Dynasty

Rinki woke next morning and knew at once that something was wrong. Even Stinki's snoring couldn't have scattered their possessions around the room like that.

"Wake up!" he honked, anxiously. "I think we've been robbed."

Dinki rummaged in her bag. "Our money has gone. And the eight-sided mirror the master gave us!"

Dinki's face went white, partly with the shock of being woken so suddenly, and partly because she knew their mission was in trouble.

"But we needed that mirror to keep the ghosts away!" Stinki moaned.

"I know," growled Rinki. "Let's go and see the innkeeper. Maybe he saw something?"

But the innkeeper had seen nothing. His wife said he had poor eyesight, which is why he had married her.

And none of the other regulars had noticed anything either.

Dinki was suspicious of the whole set-up, but kept her thoughts to herself. Without evidence, what could she do?

"If we find your missing money and your mirror we'll let you know," shouted the innkeeper, which was odd, because they hadn't told him what was missing.

"Watch out for bandits," added his wife, as the Kung-Fu Pigs prepared to leave. "There are some right villains round these parts."

Stinki vowed never to stay at a country inn again. "We've no money … and no good luck mirror. Can things get any worse?" he grumbled.

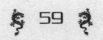

A large lump of snow slid off the roof and landed on the samurai's head.

Even serious-minded Dinki had to laugh at that!

CHAPTER 6

*"The road is long for the pig
with short legs."*
Ming-In, 3rd century

And so the Kung-Fu Pigs continued on their
journey.

CHAPTER 7

"Welcome the peace of the temple as you would welcome a weary traveller to your door."
Hi-Fi, 3rd Dynasty

As Rinki stopped for a moment to stretch his trotters he thought he saw something moving on the snowy slope ahead.

Stinki was eating a rice cake he had kept back for emergencies whilst Dinki was on her knees, meditating.

"There's someone out there!" honked Rinki, reaching for his sword.

 63

Rinki stared at the approaching figure – it looked quite real but since they were so close to the Temple of Ghosts he was taking no chances. Dinki and Stinki hurried to his side, bow and staff at the ready.

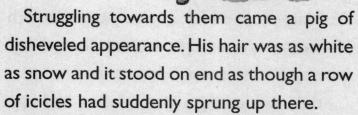

Struggling towards them came a pig of disheveled appearance. His hair was as white as snow and it stood on end as though a row of icicles had suddenly sprung up there.

This poor pig was called Xu-Glu, and his face wore an expression of terror, like someone who has had to watch Scottish football for a whole season.

Though the snow was deep, the terrified pig was running as fast as his trotters would carry him. In fact, he ran straight past the waiting Kung-Fu Pigs and it took Stinki's broad arms to stop him.

"What's the hurry, friend?" asked Stinki.

Xu-Glu didn't answer. Not with a proper sentence anyway.

"G-g-g-g-" he stammered, unable to finish his words.

"Ghosts?" asked Dinki, softly.

Xu-Glu shook his head.  "G-g-got to g-get away," he stuttered, and tried to run off again.

"Why? What have you seen?" probed Rinki.

"G-g-g-g-" whimpered the terrified pig.

"Ghosts?" asked Rinki.

Xu-Glu shook his head.

"G-g-go nowhere near th-that p-place!" he continued, his eyes almost popping out of his head. "I tried to spend the night in there but I didn't even make it to my room... Th-th-there are terrible things ... g-g-g-"

"Going on?" asked Stinki.

"No, you fools ... g-g-ghosts!"

Our three heroes looked at one another and wondered for the first time whether their mission might not be impossible after all.

They offered Xu-Glu a cup of tea but the poor chap was too far gone even for a brew. In the end they had to let him leave and he wandered off into the woods, still raving like a lunatic.

It was then that Dinki spotted something lying in the snow. "An eight-sided mirror! Xu-Glu must have left it when he ran off... We can use this instead of the one that got stolen."

"That gives us half a chance," frowned Rinki. "But do we want to end up looking like that tomorrow morning?"

Dinki looked serious. "I don't want a beard, that's for sure."

It took a minute before the boys realized she was joking.

Stinki looked up at the Temple of Ghosts, now lit by a sinister, glowing moon.

"Well ... no point in feeling sorry for ourselves. We made a promise to the emperor. Let's go!"

CHAPTER 8

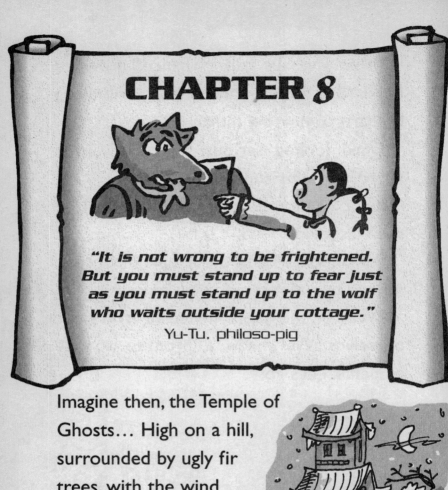

*"It is not wrong to be frightened.
But you must stand up to fear just
as you must stand up to the wolf
who waits outside your cottage."*

Yu-Tu, philoso-pig

Imagine then, the Temple of
Ghosts… High on a hill,
surrounded by ugly fir
trees, with the wind
blowing through its
open windows, then
moaning down
empty corridors.

Little flurries of snowflakes racing across the bare garden. Every door, shutter, or floorboard seeming to creak.

"As welcoming as a slap on the chops with a wet kipper," thought Stinki, as they pushed open the huge timber door.

It was early evening and not a single lantern had been lit within. The only light was from the moon and even that was occasionally hidden by cloud.

"Hello?" called out Rinki, hopefully. "Anyone at home?"

The dark courtyard seemed deserted. As empty as a peasant's wallet.

"There should be someone here," whispered Rinki. "Someone to supervise the challenge. Let's try inside."

They walked across the courtyard towards a smaller door. Dinki noticed there were footprints in the snow. Two sets.

One set would have belonged to Xu-Glu, but whose were the others?

Stinki pushed open the door. "Hello?" His voice echoed down icy corridors. "Not so much as a ghost in sight."

It was then that Rinki felt a clammy trotter on his shoulder. He leapt into the air, his heart thumping fifty to the dozen.

AHHH!

"Can I help you?" asked a quavery voice.

The three pigs spun round. An elderly pig loomed before them. He was the caretaker of the temple and his name was Heebi-Ji-Bi.

"You gave us a shock," grumbled Stinki. "Do you always creep around like that?"

"Yes," answered the caretaker. "It's a bad habit, I know. You're here to try and win the treasure, I take it?"

The Kung-Fu Pigs nodded.

"You shouldn't bother. You probably won't leave here alive. Many have tried and none succeeded. I've 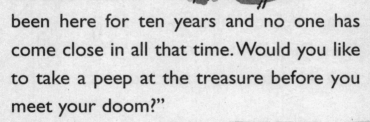 been here for ten years and no one has come close in all that time. Would you like to take a peep at the treasure before you meet your doom?"

Rinki and Stinki nodded their heads
eagerly.

Heebi-Ji-Bi led them down a set of rickety
old stairs, then fumbled
for a huge metal key
hanging around his waist.
He opened the door
and there, in the gloom,
the Kung-Fu Pigs could
see a horde of fabulous
treasure. Everything
from Ding Dynasty vases
to a third century plastic duck.

"Don't get too excited," sniffed the caretaker. "You won't be seeing it again."

Did these gloomy words put off our heroes? Of course not, for they had promised the emperor, and besides, they had the wise advice of their guru, Oinky No Ho, to guide them.

"Show us to our room," announced Rinki. "We aren't afraid of your dire warnings."

The old caretaker gave a shrug of his shoulders and lit a red lantern. "Suit yourselves. Follow me."

The room was small and damp. Stinki asked if they could keep the lantern.

"I'm afraid not. I am not allowed to help you in any way. I will return at daybreak. If you are still in your room and still alive, the treasure will be yours. Sleep tight."

Dinki volunteered to keep watch first. Stinki's eyes were already heavy, for they had walked many miles that day. Rinki told Dinki to wake him in a couple of hours when he would take his turn at the watch.

Outside, the snow fell and a passing cloud made the moon vanish.

CHAPTER 9

"Why did the oxen cross the road?
Because the road was there
to be crossed."
Emperor Bing, 4th century

For a while there was nothing to concern Dinki. Stinki snored as usual. Rinki was asleep too. Gusts of wind rattled the shutters.

But then she heard voices.

Come and dance with us!

Come and take a twirl!

Dinki guessed it was the temple ghosts come to challenge her. She glanced across at her sleeping companions. If she could defeat the ghosts alone, she thought, so much the better.

Noble Dinki, always thinking of others!

Using her fighting staff to guide her in the darkness, Dinki left the room and followed the sound of whispered voices. Each room in the temple led out on to a central courtyard, and that is where she now found herself.

Whoosh!

A ghost dressed all in strange, dusty robes swept past her and she had to quickly duck down to avoid being attacked.

Whoosh!

Another sped past in the opposite direction.

"So ... there are two of them," Dinki said. Dressed, from what she could see, in their original burial clothes from the Ding Dynasty – two hundred years ago! That would explain their weird, ethereal complexions and the foul smell which now reached her snout.

"I come in peace," began Dinki, who always preferred to avoid a fight if possible. She gasped as a machete whizzed past her left ear.

"Mmmm … so you don't want to talk!"
she whispered.

The two ghosts now mounted a joint
attack. They hopped jerkily towards her,
their stiff arms outstretched, whilst at the
end of their long white hands were nails as
sharp as knives.

Dinki leapt into her favourite Blind Tiger
Defence…

...And she darted out of the way just in time as one of the ghosts lunged at her.

It was time to try out the teachings of her wise old master. She rushed back to the doorway where she and her companions had left their travel things. Luckily the broom was still there. She grabbed the unlikely weapon.

Now to test Master's theories!

At first the ghosts didn't seem worried.
Their eyes grew redder and their green
teeth glowed in the darkness as they
flew towards her.

Dinki stood her ground
and waved the
broom in their
direction.

Suddenly the two spooks crumpled and then vanished. Their angry hissing echoed around the courtyard.

The ghosts had been defeated and Dinki felt it was time for Rinki to take the watch. She returned to the room and modestly told Rinki things had been quiet. Within seconds she was in a deep sleep.

Rinki paced the floor. Every little sound had his nerves on edge.

But suddenly he heard something else. Someone – or something – was on the roof. Rinki hurried to the window, which was open ... its shutter flapping in the breeze. The brave young warrior gripped his sword in his teeth and then clambered out into the freezing night air.

Seconds later, a hopping ghost came bouncing towards him, its lifeless features stretched into an evil smile, twenty centimetre-long nails extended like dragon's claws…

Unlike the gentle priestess, Rinki was in no mood for talking. He brandished his sword.

Swish!

The hopping ghost rushed him from out of the moonlight.

Rinki danced to one side as wise Oinky No Ho had taught him, and then crouched into his favourite fighting position: the Two Dragon Slice.

Again the blood-curdling ghost shot

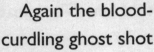

towards him. Rinki parried the charge with his sword, but then slipped. The roof was covered with snow and Rinki slithered out of control towards the edge...

He-lllp!

"Tchup!" Rinki planted his sword into the timber roof and it stopped our hero in his tracks. He could still see the ghost hovering, ready to attack. Rinki tried to remember what Oinky No Ho had told him. "To defeat a hopping ghost you must…"

No time! The spook made a third attack, and now Rinki didn't even have a sword with which to protect himself. He could see cruel fingernails crawling menacingly towards him…

Rinki racked his brain and Oinky No Ho's voice filled his head...

To defeat a ghost you must place a red and yellow death blessing on the ghost's forehead.

Rinki grabbed the blessing and hauled himself up on to the roof. "Slap!" – he got the ghoul right between the eyes. But could he remember the blessing? Rinki cast his mind back. He wished he'd listened more closely... The ghoul began to stir again, time was running out.

Take this ghost! It's in the post...

No ... that's not it, er...

In an instant the spook turned to dust and vanished, leaving only a foul smell and a last angry curse: "We will get you! You will never live to see the dawn!"

And from out of the darkness more ghosts came rushing. Lifeless but terrifying, and ready for a fight...

CHAPTER 10

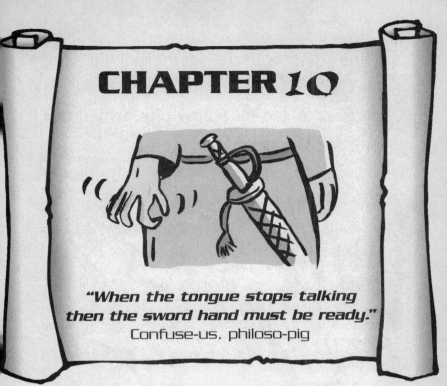

*"When the tongue stops talking
then the sword hand must be ready."*
Confuse-us, philoso-pig

The sounds of struggle coming from the roof had by now woken the other two Kung-Fu Pigs. They hurried to help Rinki, hoping that they weren't too late. Stinki couldn't believe that he had missed a battle already.

Someone could have woken me!

The ghosts had gathered in the courtyard, watched by a worried Rinki. He was glad to see his fellow pigs, armed and ready for the struggle.

They bowed to one another as Oinky No Ho had taught them and wondered if they would survive the night. The moon had by now broken through the clouds once more and bathed the temple in a silvery light.

"A fine night for spook-bashing," growled Stinki, his bow at the ready. A large and fearsome hopping ghost loomed before him, its tongue hanging down almost to its chest, and long fingernails flexed for action. Stinki fired his arrow, which of course flew straight through the ghost without harming it.

"Remember our master's instructions!" shouted Dinki, urgently, and leapt at the ghost with her straw broom. The ghost retreated in a cloud of foul-smelling dust.

Stinki now recalled Oinky No Ho telling him something about needing special weapons to take on the hopping undead. Dinki had her broom, Rinki had a red and yellow death blessing.
What was left for him?

Long-grained rice.

Stinki remembered the bag of rice, which by some miracle he hadn't yet snaffled. He rushed into the room and grabbed a handful from his bag.

Not a moment too soon: a flying corpse suddenly loomed out of the darkness and he felt its claws scratch against his helmet.

Ugh!

Stinki lashed out in defence, but he found that Oinky No Ho had spoken wisely. No samurai tricks or weapons worked against the temple ghosts, only the special items they had been given.

Time to try this rice!

Quickly, the Kung-Fu Pigs got to work with the charms Oinky No Ho had given them. Stinki was the first into action.

Rice!!!

Mmm... Those spooks really don't like this stuff!

Meanwhile, Dinki had her trusty broom.

HAAA!
More rice, you fiends!!

Mirror time!!

Rinki shone his eight-sided mirror and hoped it would work.

It did!

If I looked as ugly as those spooks I probably wouldn't like mirrors either!

Whatever the spooks tried, the Kung-Fu Pigs had an answer.

For several hours the battle raged, but now the Kung-Fu Pigs had the upper trotter. It seemed the temple ghosts could take no more, for even the dead grow weary. Their numbers had dwindled and those that were left were gathered in a sad jumble by the courtyard door.

"Please spare us," one of them murmured, its red eyes cast downwards.

"No way!" spluttered Stinki. "You tried to kill us!"

But Dinki made the samurai put down his weapons.

"Has Oinky No Ho not taught us always to show mercy?"

Stinky scuffed the earth with his boot. "S'pose so."

Rinki didn't feel like sparing the ghosts either, but he knew Dinki was right.

The Kung-Fu Pigs lowered their weapons and hoped that the ghosts really were defeated. The fight had been long and hard, on both sides, and the temple ghosts were in no mood for trickery. They knew they had lost. A one-eyed ghost dressed all in black drew Dinki to one side.

"You have been kind to us, honourable priestess. You are a pig of honour, so I must tell you something…"

Rinki wondered if it was news of the treasure, but it wasn't. It was something that would shake the Kung-Fu Pigs to the bottom of their trotters…

CHAPTER *11*

"Bad news travels faster than good news. That is the way of the world."
O-No, travelling musician, 3rd Dynasty

The Kung-Fu Pigs gathered round to hear the one-eyed ghost tell his tale.

"You are here to win the temple's treasure. It is the only reason anyone comes here."

"Smart spook," thought Stinki.

"Tell us something we don't know," muttered Rinki.

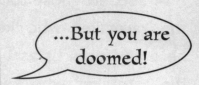

...But you are doomed!

"What treachery is this?" shouted Rinki, angrily. He reached for another death blessing.

The ghost didn't flinch, but continued his story. "It is not us who will prevent you leaving. It is the caretaker."

"The caretaker?" laughed Stinki. "What has he got to do with anything?"

A second ghost took up the tale. "It is the caretaker who keeps us imprisoned here and uses us as his private army. It is the caretaker who keeps all the treasure for himself. The caretaker is the real reason why no pig ever leaves here alive!"

Stinki shook his head angrily. "I've never heard such rubbish. We've met the caretaker. He was a bit creepy, but he was old. I can't see him causing trouble, he's a bit past that sort of thing…"

Rinki was prodding at Stinki's arm. When the samurai looked up he saw before him a most unexpected sight. It was the caretaker. But he was no longer disguised as an old man ... he was a fully fledged warrior-pig, armed to the teeth!

"You!" gasped Dinki. "Have you never heard of fair play?"

The caretaker's sword almost parted her pigtails in the middle by way of reply.

"The treasure is mine, you prying pigs, and now you must perish like petals before the icy wind!"

Dinki's eyes flashed in anger. "But what about the challenge? We have won the treasure fair and square!"

The caretaker laughed. "Finders keepers, losers weepers! The treasure is mine. And all who come to seek it must face my wrath!"

Rinki leapt into his Celestial Panda Chop position. This was going to be a tough fight for the Kung-Fu Pigs, who were exhausted from their battle with the temple ghosts.

Hah!

The caretaker loomed menacingly…

He too was an expert in the martial arts.

But Rinki parried.

While Dinki chopped.

Huh?

And then something flew through the air.

It was the ghosts who finally helped overcome the evil Heebi-Ji-Bi. They flew past and distracted him. And when he turned to fight them off, Stinki was able to land a blow on the crooked caretaker's bottom.

He toppled over
and then disappeared
down the well-shaft, his cry
echoing all around the courtyard as he fell:

(You can tell it was a deep well because he had time to say quite a bit before he hit the bottom.)

The Kung-Fu Pigs bowed to one another and then to the temple ghosts who had helped them.

CHAPTER 12

"The familiar path to the home trough ... is that not the sweetest journey in the world?"
Y-I, celebrity goatherd, 2nd century

Before departing with the treasure, the Kung-Fu Pigs had one task left to undertake. Dinki now knew that the caretaker had kept the temple ghosts there against their will. He had spread garlic around all the doors and windows to stop them leaving. (Hopping ghosts are like vampires, they don't like garlic.)

He used them to guard the treasure and frighten all who came to the temple. In the morning he would finish his guests off in person. The poor temple ghosts would never find peace until they were able to find a true resting place. They could only find this in their home village. So Dinki decided to release them from the temple by clearing away the lines of garlic from around the doors and windows.

So now we're doing housework too!

Ah, the emperor! What had he been up to while the Kung-Fu Pigs were battling away on his behalf? Well, he had been working hard as ever, looking after the kingdom.

From the Emperor's diary

11 am	get up
12 am	Lunch
4 pm	Nap
5 pm	Story from Nanny Snackette
5.55 pm	Business: Signing Executions etc
6 pm	Dinner
6.10 pm	Supper
8.30 pm	bedtime. Story read by Nanny
8.45 pm	Lanterns out, sleep!!!

CHAPTER 13

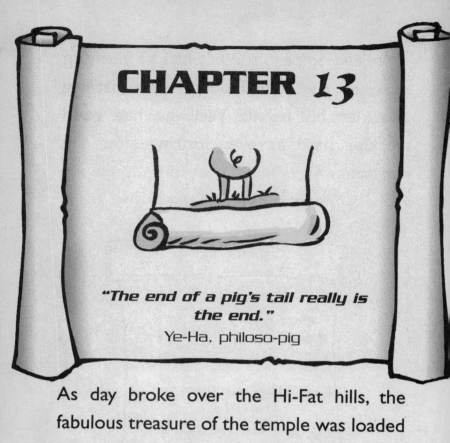

"The end of a pig's tail really is the end."

Ye-Ha, philoso-pig

As day broke over the Hi-Fat hills, the fabulous treasure of the temple was loaded into carts, ready for the long journey north.

The morning sunshine was already melting the snow and the Kung-Fu Pigs were in good spirits. (As were the good spirits in their graveyard at Jim-Jam.)

Rinki sent a messenger pigeon to the emperor telling him the welcome news that the treasure was on its way.

Later, at the Palace of the Five Happinesses, the emperor received news of his treasure. He was as excited as only a small excitable emperor can be.

"Lovely treasure! Lovely treasure!" he squeaked to all who would listen, and only stopped when the excitement brought on an attack of hiccups. His nanny told him he must calm down, at least until the treasure arrived.

"You're right. Hic. Nanny. Hic. Let us go to the throne room. Hic. And see where I can send the Kung-Fu Pigs next. Hic."

EPILOGUE

And so, brother and sister pigs, the Kung-Fu
Pigs brought treasure to the emperor, and
our great and powerful Ping-Pong was able
to celebrate with a huge banquet. That
night, the royal nanny, Manki Hanki, read
him a fairy story and tucked him into his
bed beneath fine new silk sheets. All was
well with the kingdom again, thanks to
those noble warriors, Rinki, Dinki, and
Stinki.

But now the bell tolls and I must drink
the soup of wisdom from the bowl of
enlightenment, for it is late. Go in peace, my
friends.

THE END